“Right,” said Old Sam. “Off you go then . . . send my cart home when you’ve finished with it.” He gave them a cheery wave.

As he went back into his house he gave a backward glance over his shoulder. He was smiling a secret smile, as though he knew something they didn’t.

The cart was very heavy now that it was loaded and like any other wheelbarrow, whether it be small, or large like this one, the back legs had to be lifted off the ground before it could be pushed.

Will couldn’t manage it on his own. Neither could Pa. They would have to take a handle each and do it between them. Somehow, that made it very difficult to push the cart in a straight line. It seemed to have a mind of its own.

If they tried to push it along the middle of the road, it veered immediately to one side and tried to go through the hedge. If they tried to push it along the side of the road it immediately crossed over to the opposite side, whether there was anything in the way or not, and more often than not there was.

Once it had got somewhere it didn't stay there. It turned about and went somewhere else. It was very contrary. And very difficult to push.

Pa and Will got very hot, and perspired a lot. They got rather tired and the tiniest bit cross. That feeling wasn't helped when passersby stopped, and nudged one another, and then went on their way grinning.

Just as they were about to give up and unload the cart and start carrying the wood home on their shoulders, they suddenly got it right.

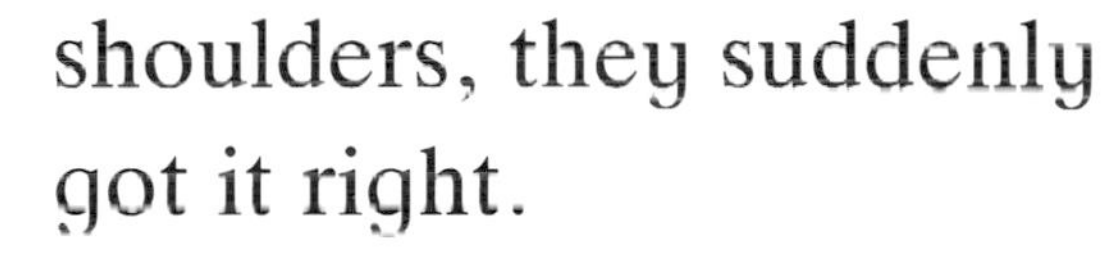

The cart started to go along the middle of the road without the slightest wobble to the left or to the right. It went so smoothly they hardly had to push it at all.

"It has decided to behave itself," sighed Pa with relief.

"And about time too," said Will.

They came to a place where the road divided.

"Together now," said Pa, "Pull towards the right."

They both pulled hard on the handles of the cart. The cart should have turned. It didn't. It stayed exactly where it was. Pa and Will were already turning. They couldn't stop themselves turning. There was only one place to go. They collided and fell to the ground.

"What happened?" gasped Will as they picked themselves up.

"You pulled the wrong way . . . you pulled to the left," said Pa crossly.

"No I didn't," said Will.

"You must have done," said Pa. "Do it properly this time."

Again they both pulled to the right. Again the cart stayed exactly where it was. Again Will and Pa fell to the ground.

"It's got a spell on it . . . ," gasped Will.

"It's in a rut," laughed a passerby, who had been watching their predicament. "Old Sam's cart always manages to find that rut. Doesn't matter who is pushing it, it always finds that rut. Been doing it for years. Surprised you didn't know about it."

And sure enough, when they looked the wheel of the cart was in a deep rut that ran along the middle of

the road like a dried up riverbed. Wheel and rut fitted together perfectly. It was as though they had been made for one another. In a manner of speaking they had. The wheel of Sam's cart had gone that way so many times before it had worn the rut in the road itself.

"That explains why it was running so smoothly," said Pa.

"It can't stay there," said Will. "We will have to lift it out."

Pa and Will heaved, and pushed and pulled. The rut was too deep and the cart too heavy. They couldn't move it at all.

"We'll have to unload everything first," sighed Pa.

He began to untie the rope holding the wood in place.

"There is no need to do that," said one of the passersby who had stopped to watch the fun.

"And what can we do instead?" asked Will impatiently.

"Stand to one side . . . ," said the passerby mysteriously.

"What's he going to do? Wave a magic wand," said Will who was tired of the whole business and wanted to go home.

"Do as I say," said the passerby, "and you will see."

So Pa and Will, who didn't want to unload all that wood and then load it all back onto the cart again, stood to one side and hoped there really was a solution to their problem.

What happened next was almost as good as someone waving a magic wand. Passersby suddenly came from all directions, and gathered round the cart. HEAVE! HO! They all lifted together. The cart came out of the rut as easily as a pea out of a pod. And then, just to make sure it didn't fall into another rut, everyone who had helped lift it, helped push it back to the woodshed.

Rooney saw them coming and had the woodshed door open. When the wood was unloaded everyone stayed for a chat.

"It's always fun seeing what happens when Old Sam's cart is out on the road," said one of their new friends. "We always get a good laugh out of it. It only seems fair to help out afterwards." And then, as though they hadn't already done enough to help they took the empty cart back to Old Sam.

# Visitors

It was a dark and windy night. Outside the trees were creaking and bending in the wind. They were casting strange moving shadows across the window. Inside the cups were rattling on the dresser. The carpets were rippling as draughts blew under the floorboards. Somewhere a door was banging.

Pa was fast asleep and snoring. Nothing would wake him until it was time to get up. Rooney had his tail curled around his ears. He was dreaming about summer days and fishing and heard nothing. Will was the only one awake. He put his head under the covers and tried to pretend he couldn't hear the door banging but he knew someone would have to get up and close it. He knew it wouldn't be Pa. He knew it wouldn't be Rooney. It would have to be him.

It was very dark downstairs. He could hear the hinges creaking on the woodshed door as it swung backwards and forwards. He was reaching out to pull it shut when he heard an unexpected sound near his feet.

Sniff . . . sniff . . . sigh . . . cough . . . sniff . . . sniff . . .

He peered down into the gloom. Holding onto the doorpost, and to one another, as though their lives depended on it, were three large bedraggled birds. Their feathers were so ruffled by the wind they looked like worn out feather dusters that were only fit to be thrown away.

Will got down onto his knees and peered into their faces.

"Why aren't you at home in bed?" he asked.

"Trees are no place for birds on a night like this," said the one nearest to the doorpost and therefore the most squashed.

It was blowing very hard. The birds were very windswept and they looked very cold. Will felt sorry for them.

"You had better come in," he said. "You can stay till the morning."

"Thank you sir, thank you sir," said the birds as they all tried to be first over the doorstep.

They wasted no time on conversation. They huddled together on the woodshed bench, tucked their heads under their wings, and went instantly to sleep.

Will went back to bed himself, amazed that anyone, especially three of anyone, could go to sleep so quickly.

"They must have been very tired," he thought.

When Will woke up next morning he thought at first the wind was still blowing there was so much rattling and banging going on. Then he noticed that everything outside was quiet and still. The wind wasn't blowing at all. The noise was coming from inside the house.

Pa woke with a start and sat bolt upright in bed.

"What is all that noise?" he asked. "And where is it coming from?"

"It's coming from downstairs," said Will, and quickly explained about the birds.

Suddenly in the middle of all the other noises they heard a frantic cry for help.

"That's Rooney's voice!" gasped Pa. He had leapt out of bed and was half way down the stairs before Will had even got his feet on the floor.

What a sight met their eyes. Rooney was racing round and round the woodshed, leaping over things, under things, through things, round things, with his tail streaming behind him like a banner. Two birds with brown wings and strong beaks were swooping after him trying to catch hold of his tail with their beaks.

There was another bird in the rafters shouting excited directions, "There he goes! He's under the bench! He's behind that plank!" And in between

shouting it was throwing things at Rooney.

"Stop! Stop this at once!" bellowed Pa. Will had never seen him look so stern.

Silence fell upon the woodshed like a thick blanket of snow. With a frightened squeak Rooney ran to Pa and leapt into his arms. "Thank goodness you have come," he sobbed.

"What is the meaning of this?" demanded Pa.

The three birds shook their shoulders and let their feathers fall sleekly into place.

"That animal . . . ," they said pointing to Rooney,

"sneaked in here when nobody was looking. We were chasing him out."

"But I live here . . . tell them I live here . . . ," sobbed Rooney into Pa's shoulder.

"He lives here," said Pa.

"He should have said," said the birds.

"Is this how you thank us for giving you shelter from the wind?" asked Will.

"But we were thanking you," said the birds. "We were chasing off an intruder."

There was no answer to that.

"It's all been a misunderstanding," said Pa, "and the least said about it the sooner it will be mended, but I would be obliged if, before you go, you tidy up the mess you have made."

The birds apologised to Rooney and said they were sorry they had chased him.

Rooney stayed well out of their way while they tidied up. He was taking no chances. Will didn't blame him.

"Next time you ask someone to stay the night make sure you make proper introductions," said Pa.

"Even if it means waking you up?" asked Will.

"Even if it means waking me up," said Pa.

"And don't forget me," said Rooney.

"I won't let him forget," said Pa.

"I wouldn't anyway," said Will.